BREATHING

Brian Ward

FRANKLIN WATTS
London/New York/Sydney/Toronto

Franklin Watts
96 Leonard Street
London
EC2A 4RH

ISBN: 0 7496 0343 7

Editor: Ros Mair
Series editor: Sarah Ridley
Design: K & Co
Consultant: Dr Philip Sawney

Illustrations: Aziz Khan pg 6(l), 7(t), 8,13, 16, 19, 22

Photographs: Heather Angel 24t; Chris Bonington 14t; Bubbles 10bl, 18bl, 23tr; Chris Fairclough 4t, 5br, 9b, 25b, 28b, 29tl, 29tr; Chris Fairclough Colour Library 10t, 15bl, 20b; © Coalition for a Smoke-Free City/Melissa Antonow 23tl; Robert Harding Picture Library 5t, 9t, 27c, 27br, 30t; Michael Holford 19t; Hutchison Library 14b, 21tl, 21tr, 30bl; NASA/Norman Barrett 15t; NHPA/A.N.T. 9c; Robert Opie 22bl; Betty Rawlings 27t; Rex Features 11b, 29b; Science Photo Library 7br, 17tl, 17tr, 17b, 18br, 24b, 25t, 26t; Shell Photo Service/Norman Barrett 12bl, 12br; Eileen Langsley/Supersport 10br, 11t; John Watney Photo Library 15br, 16b, 23b; ZEFA front cover, 5bl, 8bl, 8br, 12t, 18t, 21b, 26b, 28t.

A CIP catalogue record for this book is available from the British Library.

Printed in Belgium

CONTENTS

FEELING GOOD

Everyone knows the pleasure of taking a deep breath of fresh air. It sweeps away tiredness, making you feel alert and refreshed. The first deep breath of the day fills the lungs to capacity, revitalizing the blood flowing through your body, allowing it to take in greater amounts of oxygen from the air.

Efficient breathing is essential to your good health. It means that your lungs must expand to their proper air-containing capacity. Your ribcage, and the diaphragm, the large sheet of muscle beneath the lungs, are important to this process. If you are seated for most of the day, with your body bent over your work, your ribcage will be cramped; your lungs will not be able to work efficiently. Similarly, if your lungs are filled with pollutants from the air such as soot, dust and cigarette smoke, they cannot work properly, and could become diseased. That good feeling after a deep breath of *fresh* air depends on having healthy lungs, and clean healthy air in your environment.

△ Playing a wind instrument depends on being able to control your breathing very accurately. Your lungs, diaphragm, mouth, throat and lips must all work together to produce exactly the right airflow. This vibrates the reed of an oboe, or vibrates the lips of a trumpet player, to produce the sound.

◁ Breathing control is very important in swimming, when it must be co-ordinated with the times that the face is out of water. You also need to develop the trick of preventing water from going up your nose as you breathe in through your mouth. Swimming is excellent exercise which develops the lungs and breathing muscles.

◁ Industrial pollution is a serious threat to health, as people exposed to smoke and fumes inhale harmful substances into their lungs. Smoke from factories is less of a problem than in former times, because now there are strict laws to control the substances which can be discharged from factory chimneys.

◁ All children love blowing bubbles. If you blow bubbles on a very hot day they sink to the ground, because air from your lungs is cooler than the air around, making the bubbles heavier.

△ When you breathe out on a cold day, the "steam" you see from your breath is water vapour, which has evaporated from your lungs. This is one way that the body rids itself of waste water.

HOW LUNGS WORK

Air enters the body through the nose and mouth, and travels to the lungs down a tube at the back of the throat called the trachea. This airway is held open and protected by rings of springy cartilage, so you can move your neck around without shutting off the air supply. As it reaches the lungs, the trachea splits into two smaller branches or bronchi, one branch to each lung.

The lungs themselves are large spongy organs, full of branching airways. The bronchi divide into smaller bronchioles, and these in turn divide, like twigs on a tree. At the end of its journey, the inhaled air reaches tiny air sacs called alveoli. There are more

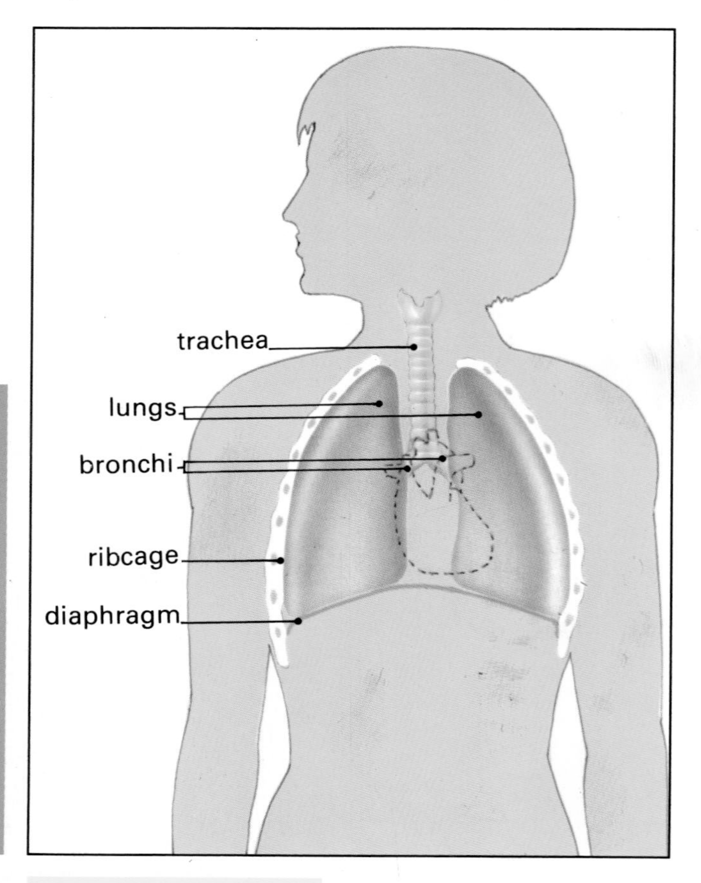

◁ The lungs are large spongy organs in the chest. They fill most of the space between the ribs. The heart lies between the two lungs, at the front of the chest. The bottom of the chest cavity is closed off by the diaphragm.

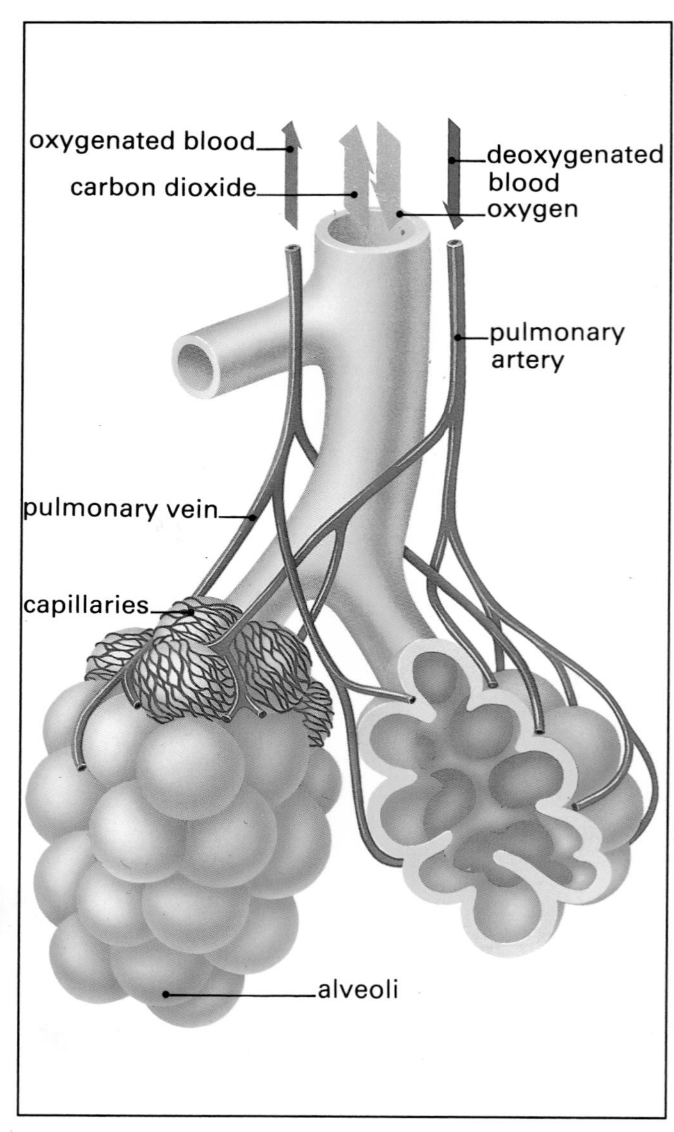

△ Air entering the lungs passes into alveoli, surrounded by capillary blood vessels. Oxygen passes through the walls of the alveoli into the blood passing along the capillaries, while carbon dioxide passes out in the opposite direction.

than 500 million alveoli; if they were flattened out they would cover an area as large as a tennis court. They have very thin walls, and are well supplied with capillary blood vessels. It is at this point, finally, that air is exchanged in the lungs. Oxygen from inhaled air passes into the red blood cells, and is carried off around the body – to be used by other cells for countless different purposes.

The airflow is also used by the larynx or voice box. As air leaves the lungs it passes over two muscular flaps, making them vibrate and produce sound. This is altered by muscles in the throat and mouth to produce speech.

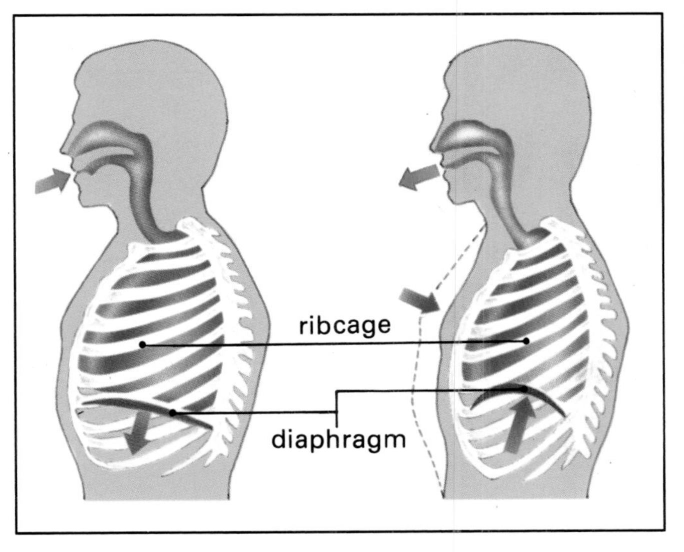

△ Air enters the lungs as the diaphragm contracts and flattens, and the ribs are lifted by muscles, enlarging the chest cavity. Used air is exhaled as the diaphragm and rib muscles relax and return to their original shape.

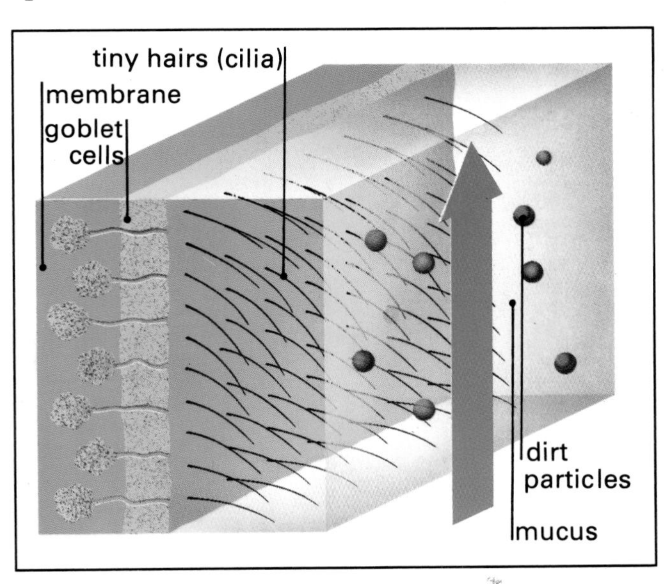

△ Inhaled dust becomes stuck in a layer of mucus lining the air passages. Tiny beating hairs in the walls of bronchioles produce a current in the mucus, carrying it and the dust up into the throat, where it is swallowed.

▷ Air enters the lungs through tubes called bronchi and bronchioles. These form a branching network called the "bronchial tree", because of its shape. The bronchioles branch into finer tubes until they end at the alveoli.

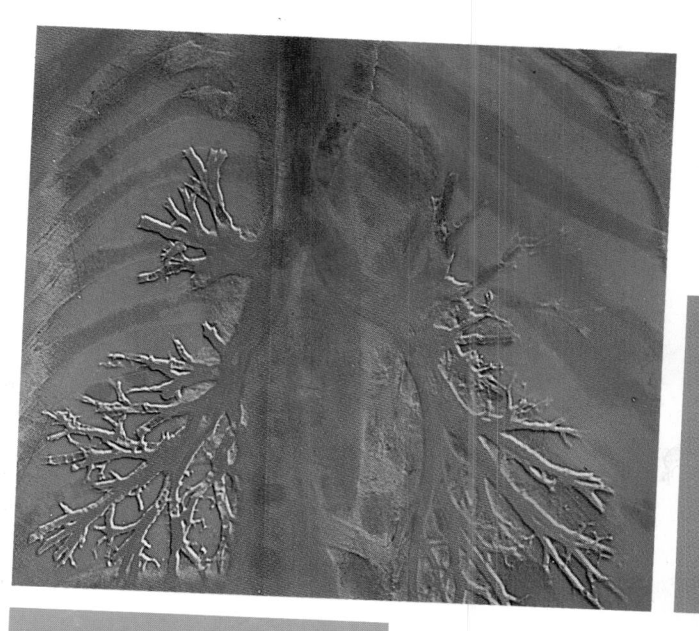

HOW YOU BREATHE

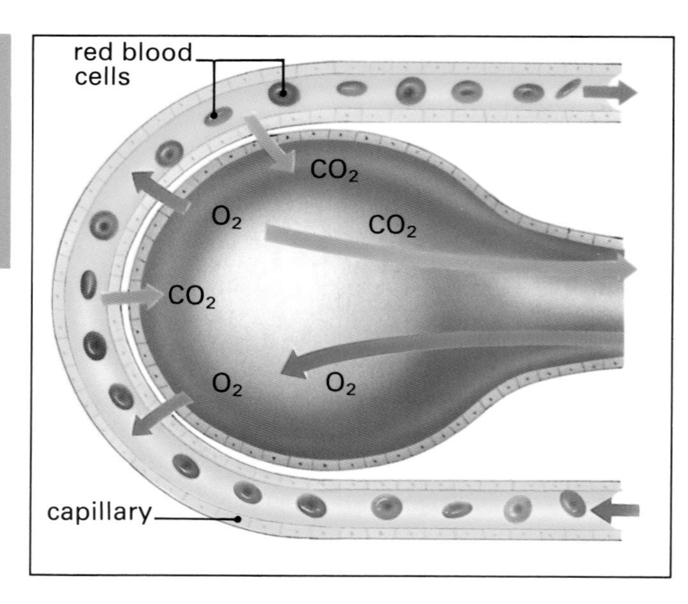

△ Oxygen is needed by all the cells in our bodies, and is obtained from inhaled air. Carbon dioxide is a waste product of cell activity, and it must be removed from the body.

▽ Breathing is an automatic process, which carries on while we are asleep.
(below right) When you blow up a balloon, you pump out about a pint of air with each breath.

Breathing is an automatic process, and no one can "forget" to breathe. It is under the control of the breathing centre in the brain stem, the area where all the other essential life processes are controlled. It is possible to control the way you breathe for a while – to breathe faster or slower, or hold your breath for a short time. But automatic processes are poised to take over. While you are asleep, breathing is regulated by the brain stem alone. You breathe less deeply because the body is producing less carbon dioxide. When you are awake and moving, your body generates more carbon dioxide, and the chemical regulation comes into play. The rate at which we breathe depends chiefly on the level of waste carbon dioxide in the blood. As this builds up, special receptor cells detect the increasing levels, and the brain produces signals that make us breathe faster and more deeply. This flushes more carbon dioxide out of the used blood, and into the

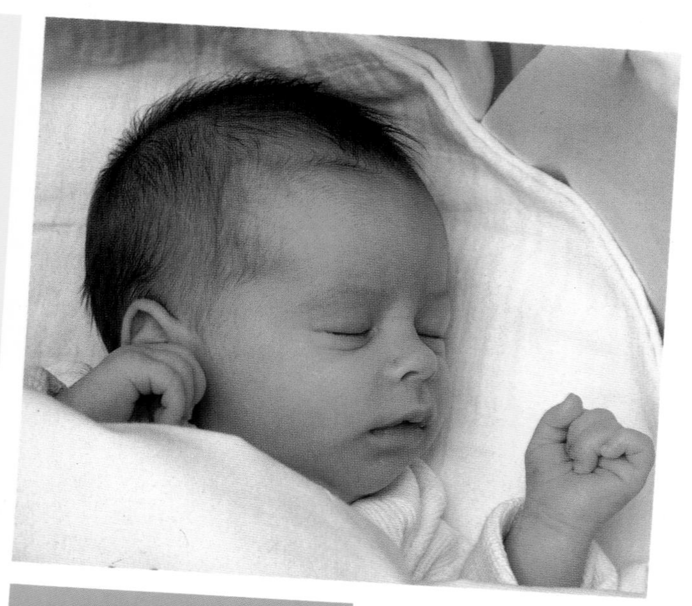

◁ Even tiny babies have enough control over their breathing to be able to swim. They hold their breath and swim under water because they are not strong enough to lift their heads above the water to breathe. At this age they do not have any fear of water. This is a strange ability, because it does not have any real function.

▷ Air-breathing marine animals, like whales, can dive to enormous depths while holding their breath. Their bodies are adapted to withstand pressure, and they divert the vital blood flow from the other organs to their brains while underwater.

▽ The peak flow meter measures the amount of air you can blow out of your lungs when you blow really hard. It is used by people with asthma to check the health of their lungs.

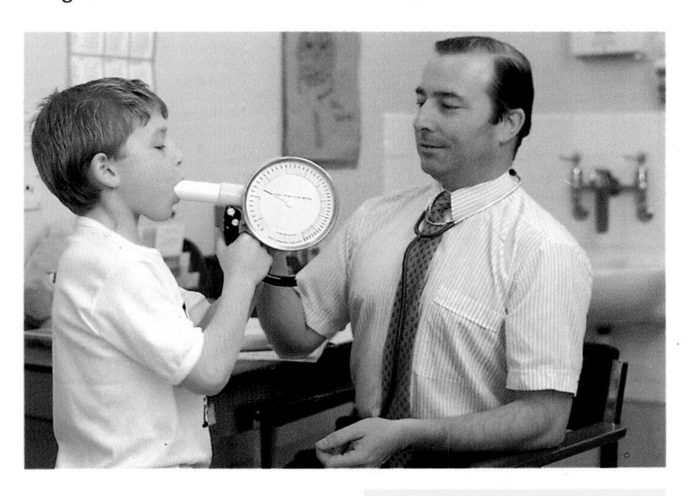

alveoli, so it can be breathed out. Once carbon dioxide levels are reduced, breathing returns to normal. This process of bringing in oxygen and removing carbon dioxide is a continuous one.

The amount of air processed is enormous. With each breath, the lungs move about one pint of air, but their full capacity is as much as thirteen pints. When we exert ourselves, the amount can rise to fifteen or even twenty times normal, using about twenty gallons of air each minute.

EXERCISE AND LUNGS

Exercise has some very important effects on the body. When you run, your breathing speeds up until you are panting and at the same time, your heart rate increases. The heart pumps blood faster to supply oxygen to your muscles, so they can work harder. But if you exercise regularly, your body's responses will change. You won't get so out of breath, and your heart won't race so much. With *regular* exercise of the right sort, your whole system learns to cope better.

Sportsmen and athletes know that they must exercise regularly. Their bodies have learned to use oxygen more efficiently. Oxygen is used to break down stored material in the body to release energy. As this energy becomes more easily available, the body can exert itself more, or gets less tired after normal sorts of exercise.

If you start fitness training, you will need to exercise every day, for about thirty minutes. Your choice of exercise must make you slightly out of breath, so that your heart beats faster. Gradually you will find that you can exercise longer, or more strenuously. Your pulse (the rate at which your heart pumps blood through your body) will get slower. Your breathing rate will also reduce. Your lungs and circulation will be stronger and healthier.

◁ Cycling is good exercise for the lungs and muscles. You need to breathe deeply and steadily when cycling long distances.

(below left) You can also benefit from work-outs in the gymnasium. This makes you supple as well as improving breathing.

▽ Hurdling means violent exercise over a short period. When this happens, oxygen is used up faster than the lungs can restore it to the blood, so the body must work without it for a short time. This is called an anaerobic condition.

Better breathing

- With regular exercise, your body learns to make better use of oxygen. After a few weeks of training, your body's use of oxygen will be 25% more efficient.
- The extra exercise and increased supply of oxygen improves the functioning of your heart and muscles.
- You will not pant so much when you exert yourself, and your pulse will not speed up as much as it used to.

◁ Marathon runners train over a long period so that their lungs and bodies adjust to taking in more oxygen, and learn to use it more efficiently. Once trained properly, they can run for many hours in a steady rhythm. They still lose water from their lungs and through perspiration, and need frequent drinks.

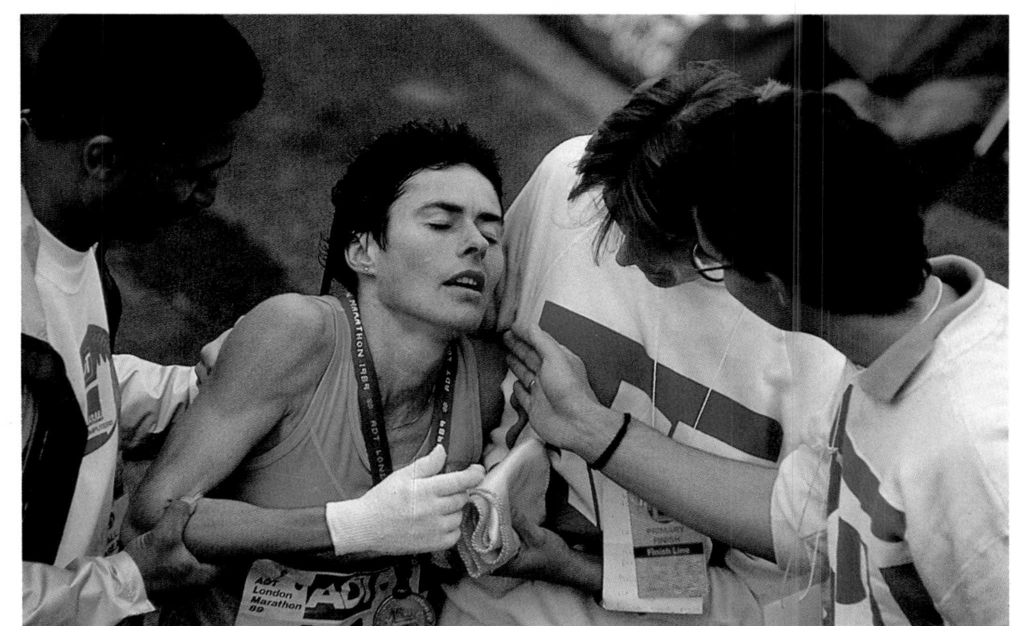

▷ With lots of training, athletes are able to continue to run or take part in other sports long after the time that normal people would be exhausted. They have trained to get through the "pain barrier" – the warning signs which tell us to rest or risk damaging ourselves. This allows athletes to continue to use up the body's reserves of energy until they may suddenly collapse, without much warning.

UNDER PRESSURE

The air around us is under pressure. Although we cannot feel it, this weight of air is pressing on our bodies all the time. If you go underwater, the pressure increases sharply with depth. Swimming with a snorkel on the surface, you are breathing air at normal pressure. If you made a long snorkel tube, however, and tried to swim around 30 cm below the surface, you would not be able to breathe at all; the pressure of water on your chest would stop you breathing in. If you hold your breath and dive down into water, similar effects of pressure against your chest soon make you uncomfortable. Scuba gear was invented to avoid this problem. Divers using it breathe air which is always at the same pressure as the water outside. Deep-sea divers encounter other hazards.

△ Breathing compressed air prevents the chest from being crushed by pressure.

▽ When scuba divers come up from great depths, bubbles may form in the blood. They must be treated in a decompression chamber to force the bubbles to dissolve again.

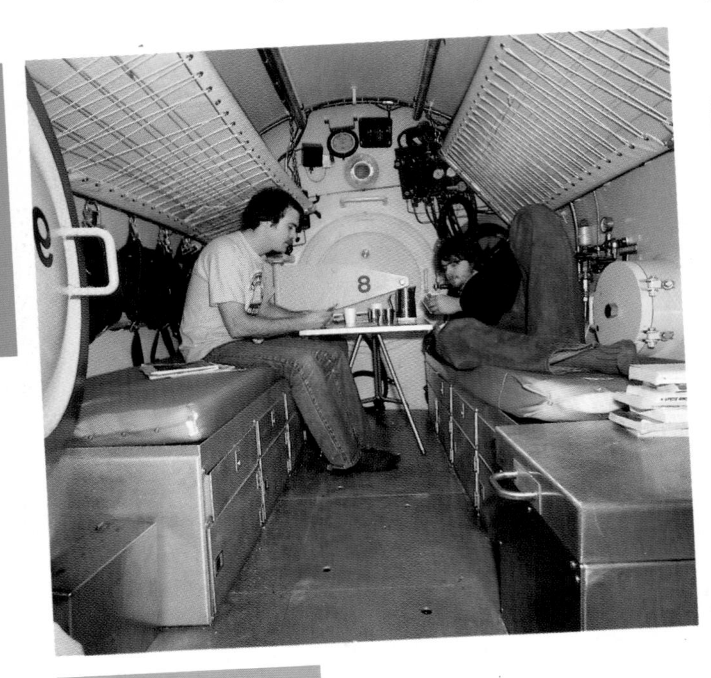

▽ Wearing an armoured suit, a diver is able to work at great depths, without being crushed.

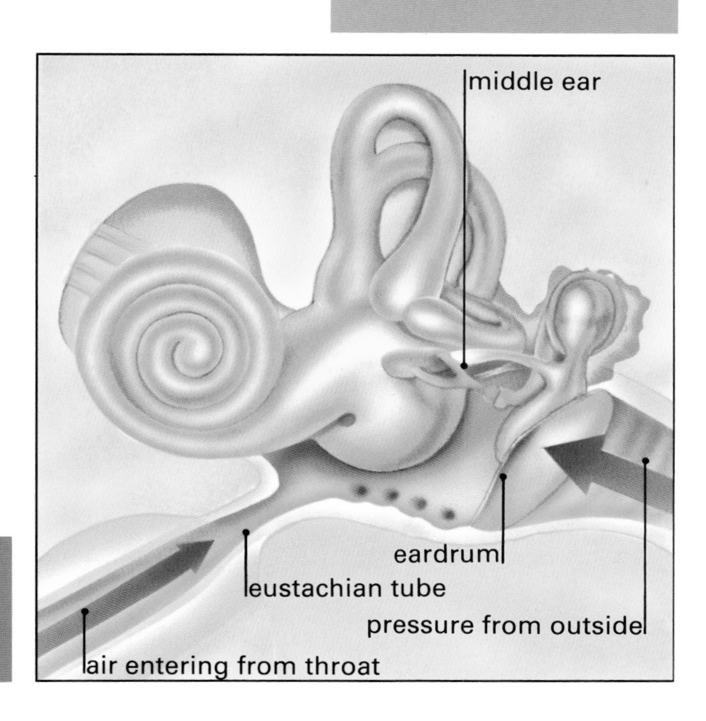

△ When air pressure increases, it presses on your eardrum against the low pressure inside.

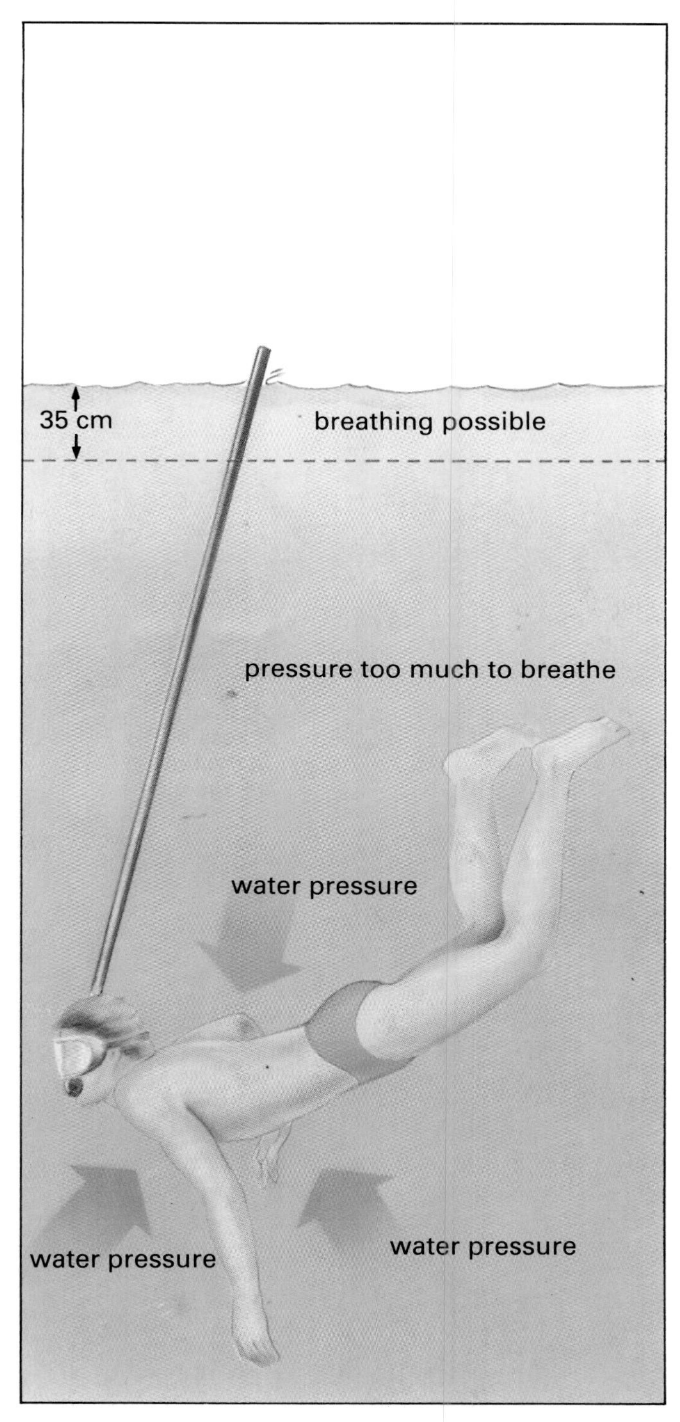

▷ Water is heavy, and presses on you harder than air. So you can't breathe through a long snorkel.

Large amounts of nitrogen will dissolve in blood under pressure. If a diver comes up too quickly, the nitrogen bubbles out of the blood like a fizzy drink, and can lodge in blood vessels or other tissues, causing a disease known as the "bends".

Pain in the ears, or in the sinuses of the face, tends to be caused by outside pressure squeezing air cavities which are blocked off, unable to release pressure. Ears are common problem areas. Pain is caused by blockage of the eustachian tube, leading from the middle ear into the throat. A cold or catarrh can block this tube, or the entrance to the sinuses, causing pain when pressure increases.

THIN AIR

Just as going underwater increases the air pressure, so going up causes air pressure to drop. If you fly in an aircraft, this drop in pressure may make your ears "pop". You may even get the same effect going up in a lift. The popping sensation is due to air inside the middle ear forcing its way out through the eustachian tube, because it is at higher pressure than the low pressure air outside. The reverse happens when an aircraft comes down again, when the increasing pressure may make your ears hurt.

Under low pressure, you need to take in more air to obtain the normal amount of oxygen. The higher you go, the more breathless you feel. If you don't get enough air, as can happen on very high mountains, your brain becomes starved of oxygen; you feel dizzy, weak and disoriented. Fortunately, however, your body can adjust to this after some time. People who live on high mountains develop larger chest cavities and have extra red blood cells so that they can take in more oxygen.

△ Air gets very thin as you go higher, and the body cannot take in sufficient oxygen. Mountaineers sometimes carry oxygen cylinders with them to use at very high altitudes, when climbing is difficult because the body is starved of oxygen.

▷ People who live high in the mountains, like these Peruvians, become accustomed to the high altitude. They develop large chest cavities in order to breathe in as much air as possible, and their blood contains extra red blood cells to carry oxygen around their bodies. It takes many years for the body to adjust to living high up.

◁ In space, there is no air at all, and astronauts have to breathe air which is carried in cylinders. Pure oxygen is too dangerous for this use.

(bottom left) Modern jet aircraft fly at high altitudes where there is very little oxygen. In passenger jets the thin air is pumped in to increase the pressure, so it is equivalent to being at a lower altitude. Most military jets are not pressurized in this way, and pilots breathe pure oxygen through an oxygen mask.

▽ As an aircraft descends, the air pressure increases. It can press uncomfortably on the eardrums, and this often upsets young babies.

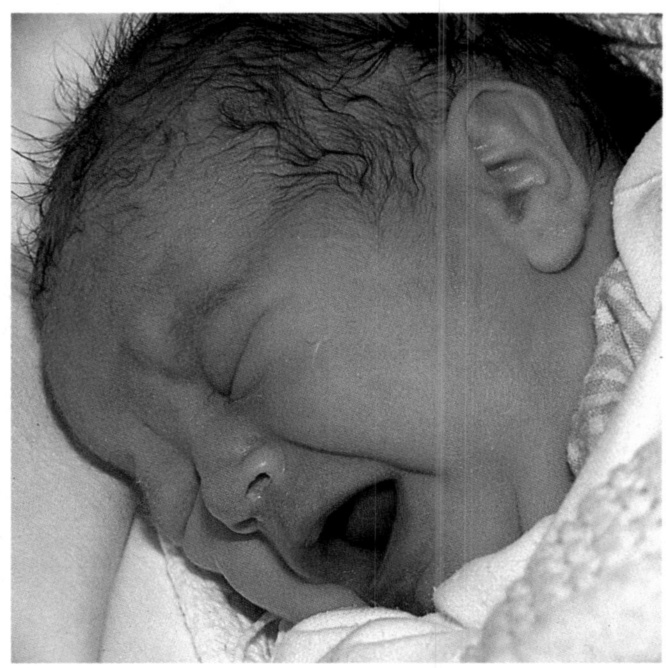

THROAT INFECTIONS

Various different types of microbes attack the parts of your body involved with breathing. Those that affect the airways between the lungs and the mouth and nose are called upper respiratory, or upper airway infections. Throat infections are very common. Those caused by bacteria can be treated with antibiotics, but they usually clear up without treatment. Virus infections are more of a problem, because there is no treatment which will kill viruses hidden inside living body cells. They too will gradually clear up naturally. Such throat infections usually last for a week or ten days, and they may make you feel hot and achy. Paracetamol at the recommended dosage will help keep your temperature down, and plenty to drink helps too.

Sometimes the affected area spreads down

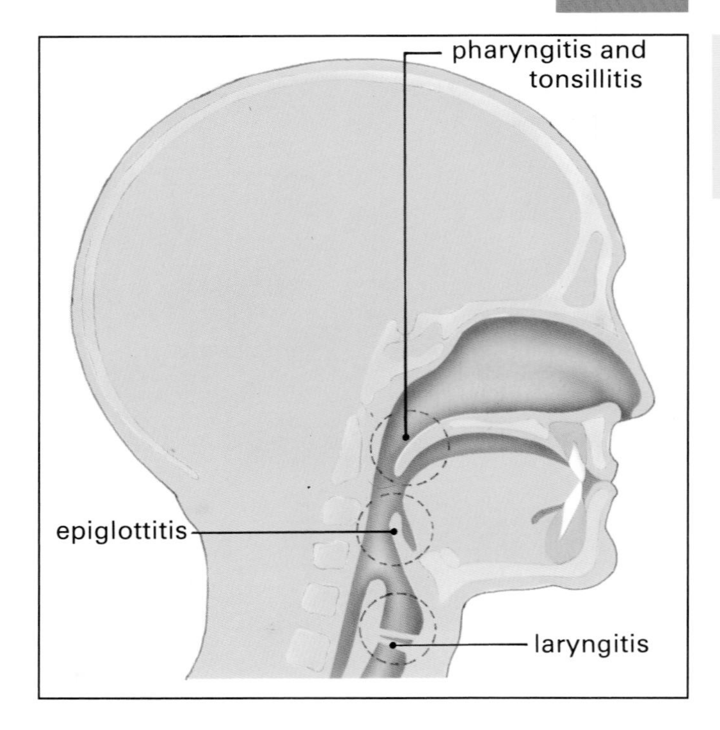

△ Several different types of infection can cause a sore throat. Almost all of the mouth, throat and upper parts of the breathing apparatus pick up these common infections, which can cause scratchy throat pain and fever.

◁ When you have a sore throat, gargling with a medicated mixture will ease the scratchiness and make your mouth taste fresher. It won't kill off the microbes in your sore throat, but your body's own defences should soon do this.

△ These Streptococci bacteria can cause sore throats. They are bacteria which can be killed by antibiotics.

to your larynx, and, when the vocal cords are involved, the inflammation makes you "lose your voice". In young children, infection of the upper airway can cause croup which produces noisy breathing and violent coughing. It is greatly eased by breathing steam (as in a steamy bathroom). Infection of the epiglottis can be very serious, as inflammation and swelling may almost close off the airway. Another common throat infection is tonsillitis, caused by viruses or bacteria attacking two patches of soft tissue at the back of the throat. Your doctor may suggest a minor operation to remove them if you suffer from recurrent tonsillitis.

△ The doctor can often tell what is causing your sore throat because of the area infected, and the appearance of your throat.

▽ In tonsillitis, the tonsils are enlarged; they may also be inflamed and covered with a white discharge.

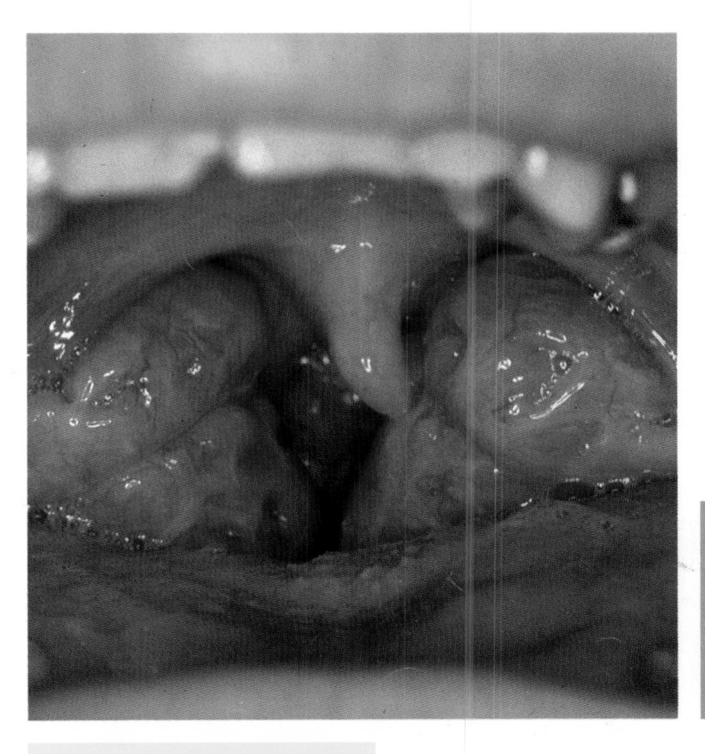

COUGHS AND SNEEZES

Coughs and sneezes are sudden exhalations of air intended to remove blockages; they may be a response to irritation or infection in the airways. They are usually caused by viruses, but sometimes bacteria attack the damaged tissues as well, causing coughing or catarrh which may linger a long time.

Of all the upper respiratory infections, the commonest are colds and influenza or 'flu. Colds are caused by different types of virus. An average attack comes with an infection of the throat and the air passages behind the nose, causing the tissues to become inflamed and painful, and stimulating them to produce large amounts of sticky mucus. A "cold in the

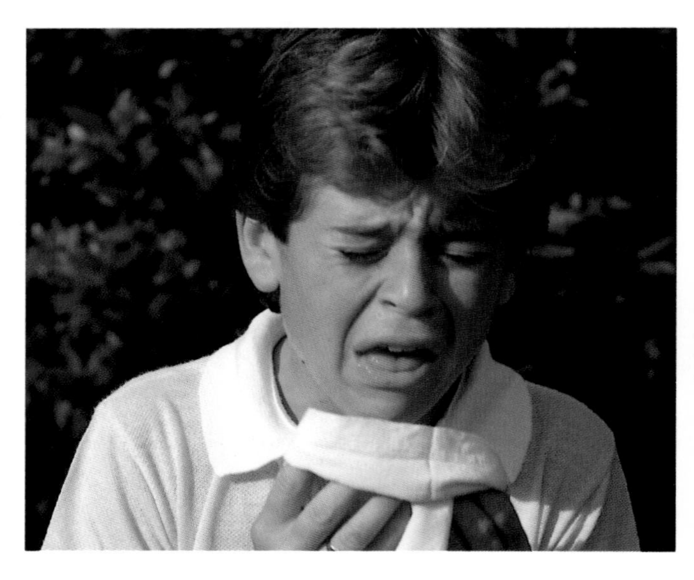

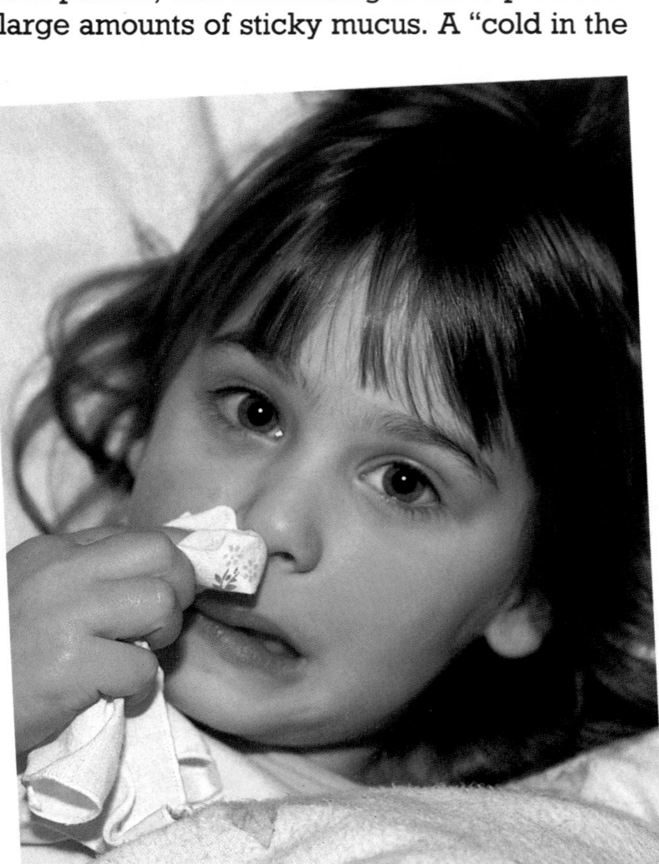

◁ A cold makes you feel very miserable. It is caused by a virus which infects the throat and nose, and sometimes the lungs too. There are lots of different cold viruses, and so far there is no way to treat the infections they cause, though you can take medicines to make you feel a bit better.

△ With one sneeze, you can blast out thousands of invisible water droplets containing viruses or bacteria which could infect other people.

▽ This pinkish blob is a mass of cold viruses reproducing inside another cell. Soon they will escape to spread the infection.

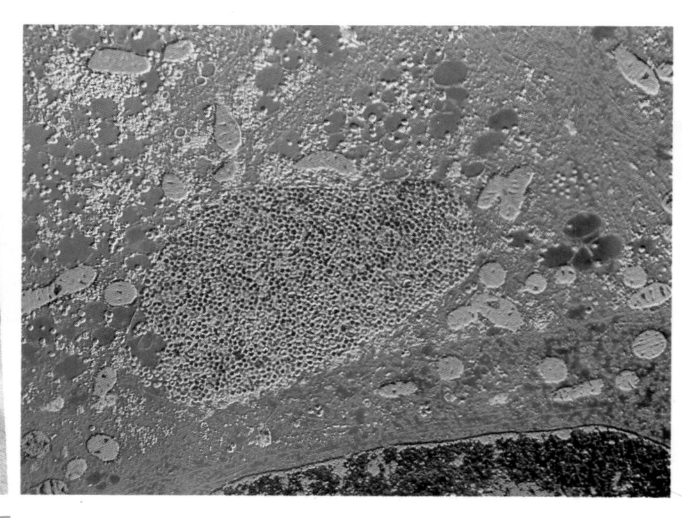

nose" causes itching, and the body responds by sneezing, which may dislodge the mucus. The sudden rush of air through the nasal passages also takes with it huge numbers of water droplets containing virus particles, which spread the disease to people who inhale them. 'Flu resembles a cold, but is more severe. It causes a high fever and makes you feel very weak; the infection often attacks the lungs, leaving them raw and making it painful to breathe for a while. A vaccine is available to give some protection against 'flu, but there are several different forms so protection is not 100 per cent reliable.

▽ A new strain of 'flu appeared in Hong Kong in 1969, and was carried around the world by air travellers. Few people had natural immunity.

▷ When the first settlers arrived in America, they brought colds and other diseases. These killed many Indians, who had no immunity to them.

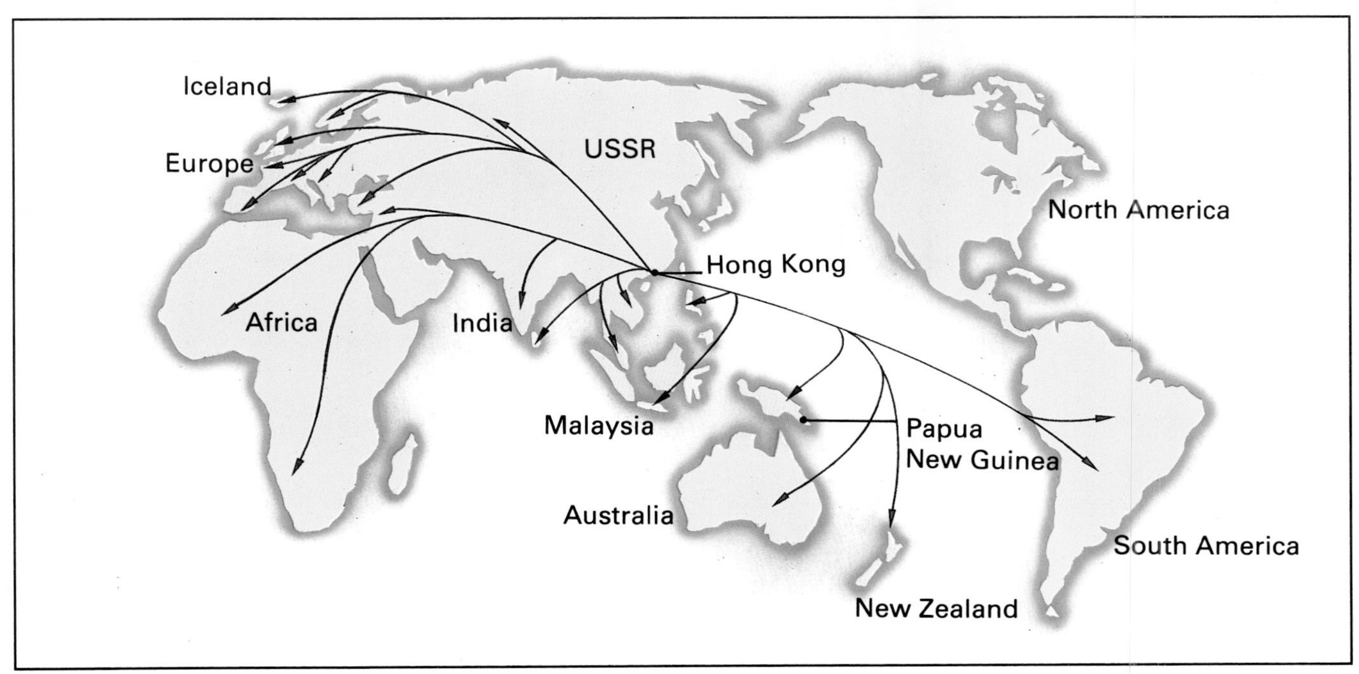

SERIOUS INFECTIONS

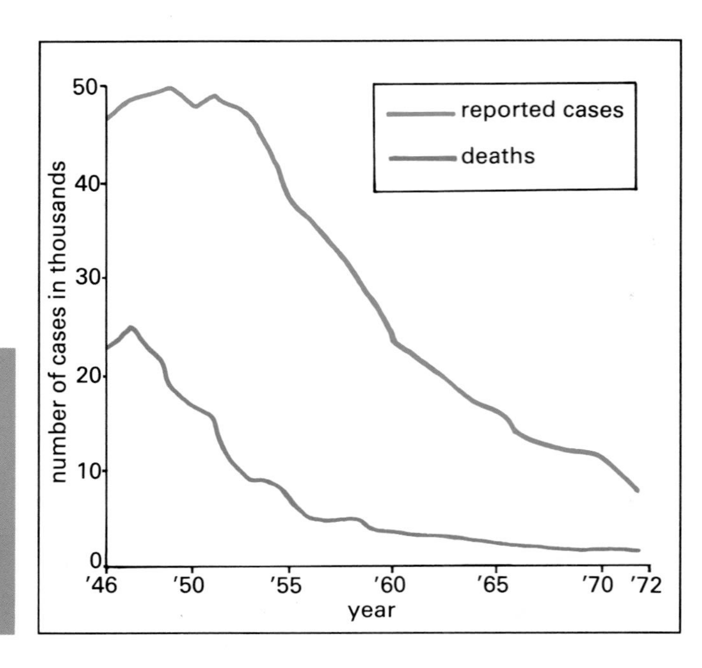

△ TB is a disease affecting people living in poor accommodation, and eating an inadequate diet. It began to disappear as living conditions improved after World War II.

Deaths also reduced quickly because effective new drugs were introduced, and a drop in the number of cases of the disease soon followed.

Some very serious diseases attack the lungs. Tuberculosis, better known as TB, is a disease caused by bacteria which damage and scar the lungs. TB is difficult to treat because the bacteria grow very slowly and antibiotics have to be taken for many months – some bacteria may remain hidden in the scar tissue, ready to cause another attack.

Pneumonia is a serious lung infection which may affect people weakened by other disease, or by old age. It can be produced by various viruses or bacteria, which cause the lungs to gradually fill with fluid. It is particularly likely to affect bedridden elderly people, and those who are weakened by poor living conditions and a poor diet.

Legionnaires' disease is caused by bacteria which grow in warm water, and is sometimes found in air-conditioning systems and showers. People who inhale infected droplets may suffer from a serious form of pneumonia, which has to be treated with exactly the right antibiotics.

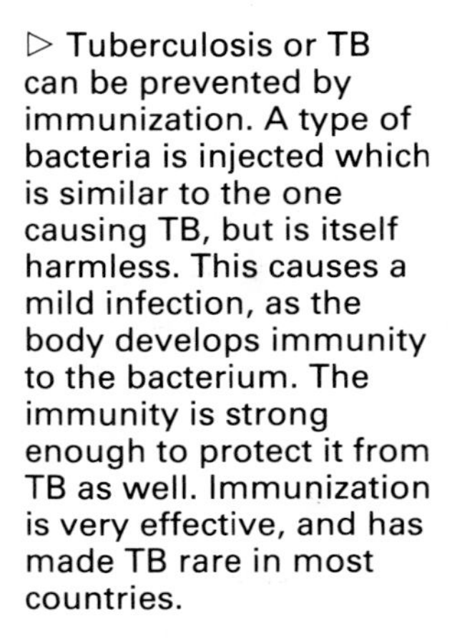

▷ Tuberculosis or TB can be prevented by immunization. A type of bacteria is injected which is similar to the one causing TB, but is itself harmless. This causes a mild infection, as the body develops immunity to the bacterium. The immunity is strong enough to protect it from TB as well. Immunization is very effective, and has made TB rare in most countries.

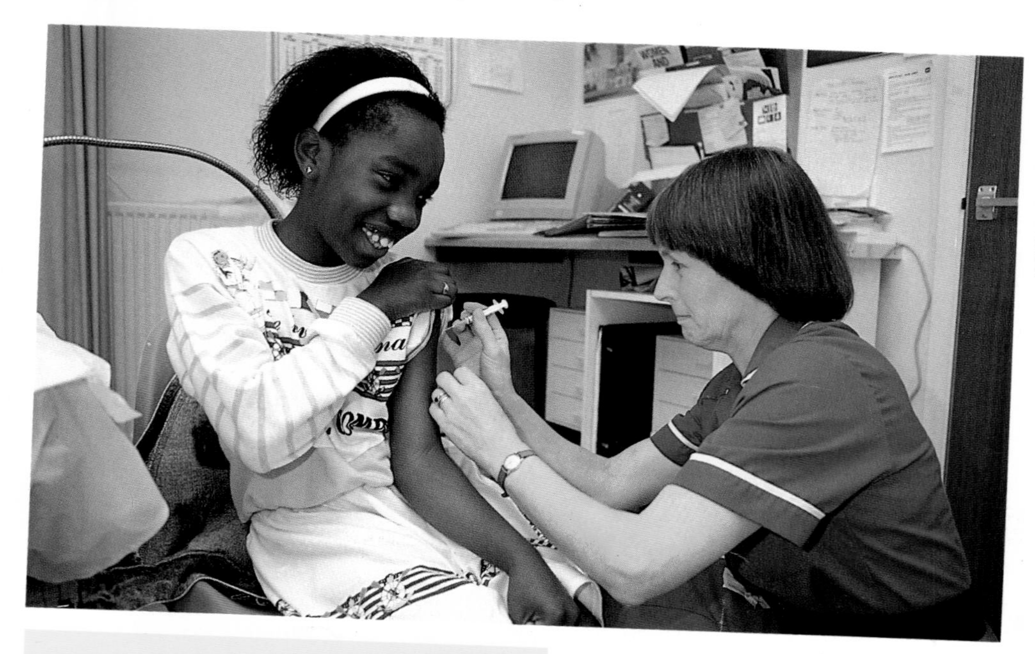

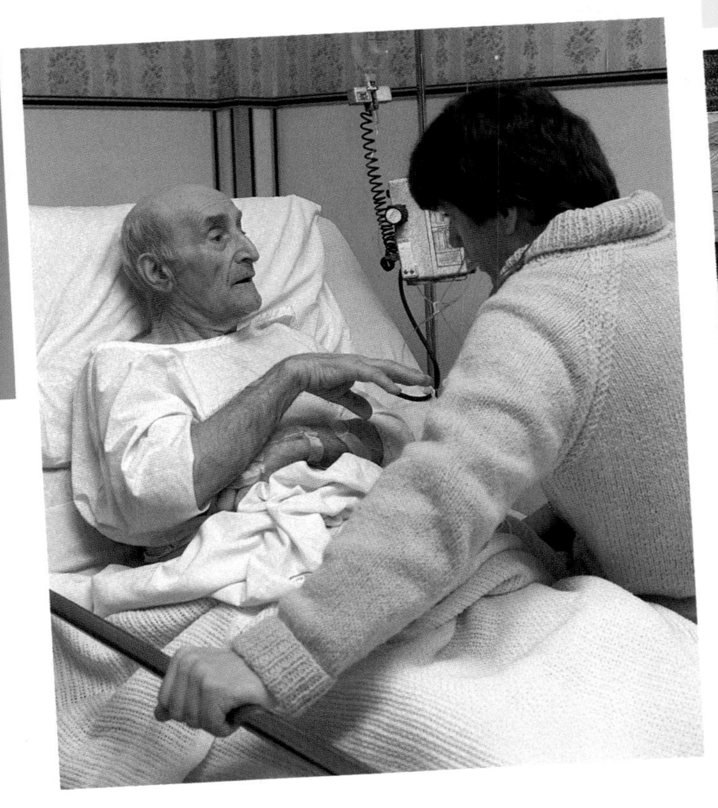

△ Old people who are weakened and bed-ridden are very susceptible to the viruses and bacteria which can cause pneumonia.

(top right) Overcrowded slum housing and a poor diet weakens people and makes diseases like TB more of a threat to health.

▷ Legionnaires' disease is caused by bacteria which thrive in hot water, and can grow and spread in hot water tanks on the roofs of buildings, and in some types of air conditioning systems. Water droplets spread the infection, which causes a type of pneumonia and may affect other organs as well.

SMOKING RISKS

Everyone now knows that smoking is dangerous, because it can cause disease of the lungs. It also damages the heart and circulation, as well as some other organs. Tobacco smoke includes tar, thick brown sticky material, which contains several substances known to cause cancer. Another constituent is soot, which is deposited in the lungs, blackening and hardening them. Carbon monoxide is also produced by burning tobacco. It is thought to cause heart disease.

Lung cancer caused by smoking is quite common, and other smokers' diseases are as serious. Bronchitis, or inflammation of the bronchi caused by smoke, can cause serious lung damage. In some long-time smokers, the lung tissue breaks down and becomes scarred, causing emphysema. The sufferer cannot absorb oxygen in his or her damaged lungs. Even non-smokers may be affected if constantly exposed to smoke, and may suffer the same sorts of lung damage. A pregnant woman smoker can cause harm to the unborn child. Smoking is addictive, like some "hard" drugs, and can be as hard to give up.

◁ In the 1950s, smoking was advertised in a way which made the habit seem healthy. Such advertising is not allowed now the risks are known.

▽ Poisons in tobacco smoke stop the beating of tiny hairs (cilia) in the airways, preventing the natural cleaning process of the lungs from removing tar and soot.

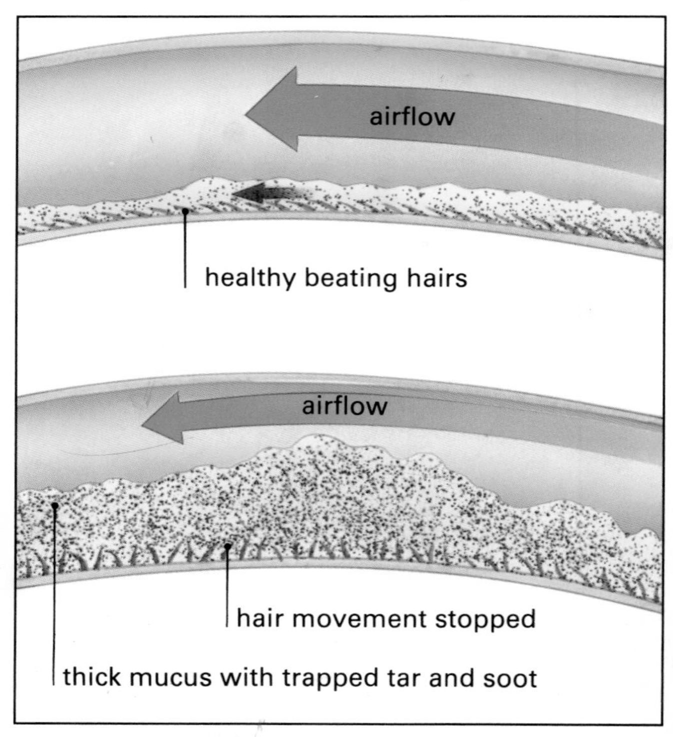

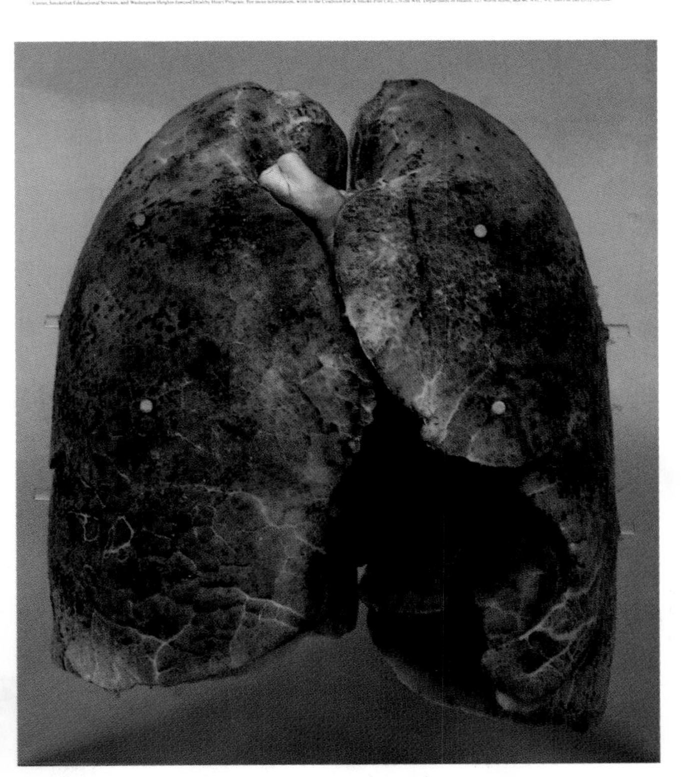

(top left) Smoking is now generally realised to be a serious threat to health. Public education posters like this underline the dangers.

(bottom left) Instead of a normal healthy pink, this smoker's lung has been blackened by the tar and soot inhaled over years of smoking.

△ Passive, or secondary, smoking describes the effects of other people's cigarette smoke on non-smokers. Passive smoking has recently been proved to be a serious health risk.

Facts about smoking

- Smoking 20 cigarettes a day will shorten your life by 5 years.
- 40% of heavy smokers will die before reaching retirement age.
- 40% of all male cancer deaths are lung cancers, caused by smoking.
- The effects of smoking on the heart and circulation kill twice as many people as lung cancer.
- Smokers take twice as much time off work through sickness than non-smokers.

ALLERGIES AND ASTHMA

The body's immune system is a complicated defence designed to protect us from harmful organisms or foreign substances which get into the body. Usually this works very well, but sometimes it can go wrong. In hay fever, the immune system treats substances like grass pollen as though they were dangerous invaders; it fights back with an allergic reaction. Fierce itching in the nose follows, and sneezing, together with red, scratchy and watering eyes. The usual treatment is with antihistamine drugs.

Asthma is a lung disease in which the smaller airways narrow and become inflamed, making it difficult to breathe and causing wheezing and coughing. Asthma is the commonest cause of continuing coughing in children. An attack of asthma may be brought on by an allergy and asthma sufferers often have allergic symptoms like eczema. Attacks can also be brought on by stress or excitement, but often there is no

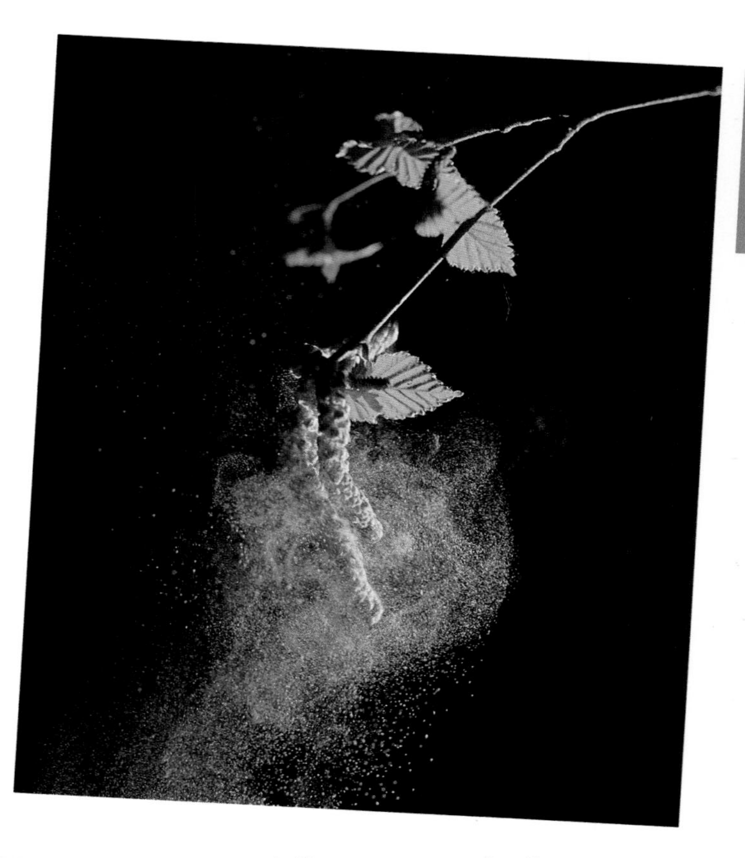

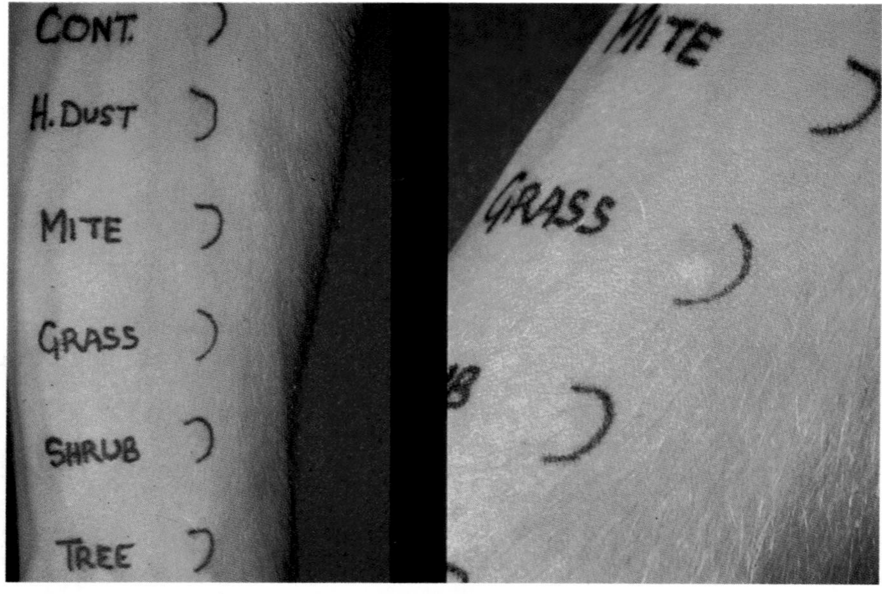

△ Huge amounts of pollen are released from birch trees in the spring. This pollen is carried in the air, and is a very common cause of hay fever allergy in Northern Europe. Grass pollen is the most common cause of hay fever so it is wise for sufferers to avoid grassy areas in early summer. Hay fever affects people even in the centre of towns, because the pollen is carried long distances by the wind.

◁ In an allergy test, substances known to cause allergies are pricked into the skin, and the reaction shows if an allergy is present. In these pictures, there is allergy to grass pollen, which has caused a small blister to develop where it was pricked through the skin. This patient will be advised to take anti-allergic drugs during the grass pollen season.

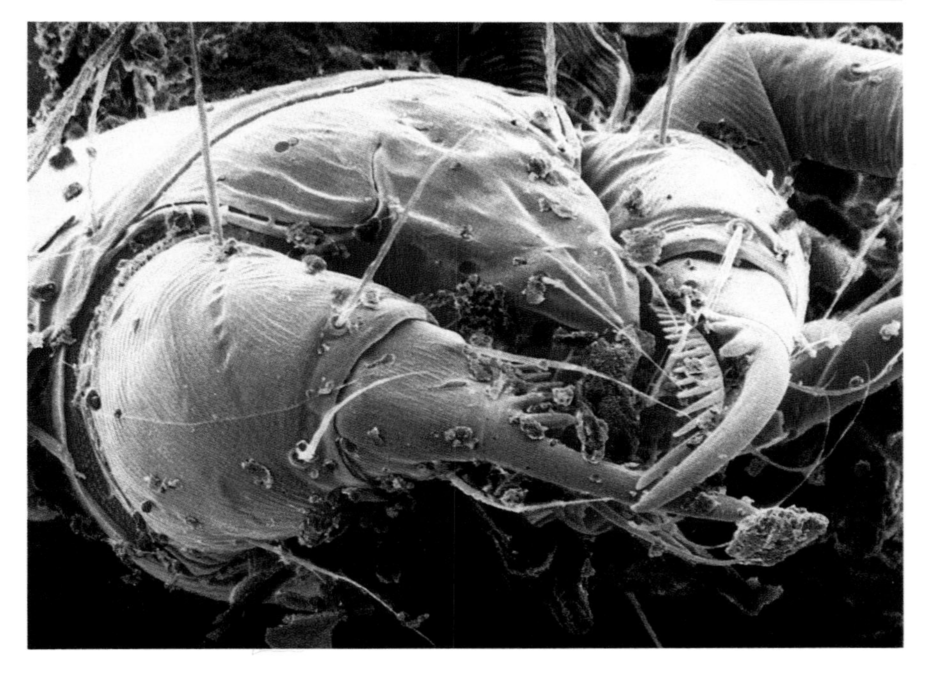

◁ A house dust mite, seen here magnified many times, lives unseen in houses, feeding on dust. It is actually the size of a speck of dust but is a common cause of allergies and asthma, especially when dust is disturbed during cleaning.

(bottom left) People with asthma often need to use an inhaler to open up the airways in the lungs and let them breathe freely. Inhalers are special devices which spray a measured amount of the drug straight into the mouth, where it is breathed directly into the lungs.

▽ In an asthma attack, rings of muscle around the bronchioles tighten, narrowing the airway. The bronchioles become inflamed and swollen, and it becomes very hard to breathe.

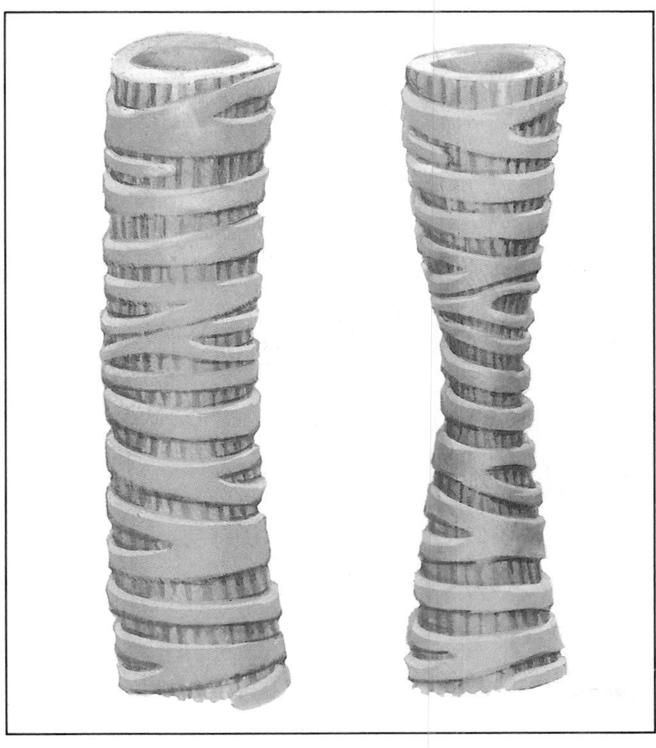

obvious cause. Sufferers are taught to use an inhaler or some other device when they have an attack. They are also often given a small meter to blow into, which shows if their asthma is under control. Drugs can be taken continuously to make attacks less likely and to maintain good health.

AIR POLLUTION

A breath of fresh air may revitalize the body, but all too often the air we breathe contains pollutants like dust and car exhaust fumes. The lungs can remove most of these materials, or make them harmless, but very polluted air may overcome the lungs' defences and cause damage. Some pollutants belong to work places: farmers' lung is caused by straw dust; asbestosis used to be common among asbestos workers.

Air pollution comes from a multitude of different sources, some unexpected. Exhausts from vehicles using leaded petrol produce large amounts of poisonous lead in the atmosphere. The lead is absorbed by children living in areas close to busy roads. Serious air pollution is also produced by many industries, and is now controlled by law. A more unusual case is the release of an unpleasant gas called formaldehyde, which

△ Asbestos workers wear protective suits and masks, to prevent inhalation of asbestos dust. This material, used for insulation, has been found to cause a rare form of lung cancer, and is now being removed from old buildings.

▷ This German power station is powered by brown coal. When this type of coal is burned it produces a lot of dangerous pollutants which can be a health risk. The smoke has to be treated to make it harmless, and this is expensive.

▷ People living in certain areas are threatened by a radioactive gas, radon. This is given off by granite rocks when they are near the earth's surface. It may collect in houses and could be a health risk but special floors and pumps can be inserted to give protection.

◁ Car exhausts produce several dangerous air pollutants including lead. Lead-free petrol is now available, and catalytic convertors are being used to cut out the most harmful fumes.

▽ Los Angeles is notorious for its smogs. These occur when car exhausts and factory fumes are affected by light, and a thick haze settles on the city. This irritates eyes and lungs.

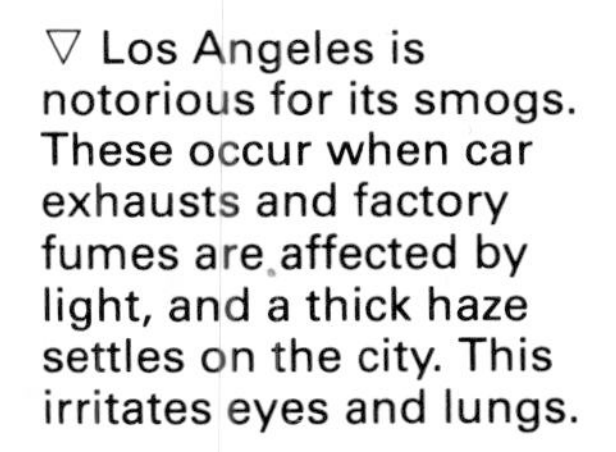

leaks out of some types of plastic foam used for building insulation, leading to sore throats and itching eyes. This is sometimes called "sick building disease". Another unusual pollutant is radon, a radioactive gas, which gradually leaks out of granite rock. People living in granite regions are exposed to minute amounts of radon, which may accumulate and cause disease.

LUNG DEFECTS

Some breathing problems are caused by defects in the lungs. This is quite common in premature babies, since their lungs may not be fully developed at birth. In such cases, the lungs lack an essential chemical called surfactant, which prevents the moist tissues from sticking together. The baby may need to be given extra oxygen. Badly affected babies are put on a machine called a ventilator, which helps them to breathe.

Cystic fibrosis is an inherited disease in which there is a fault in the chromosomes. About one person in every twenty-five carries the affected gene, although they are not affected by the disease. If two of these "carriers" have a child, there is a one in four chance that it will be affected by the disease. Among other serious problems, the lungs become clogged with sticky mucus, which is

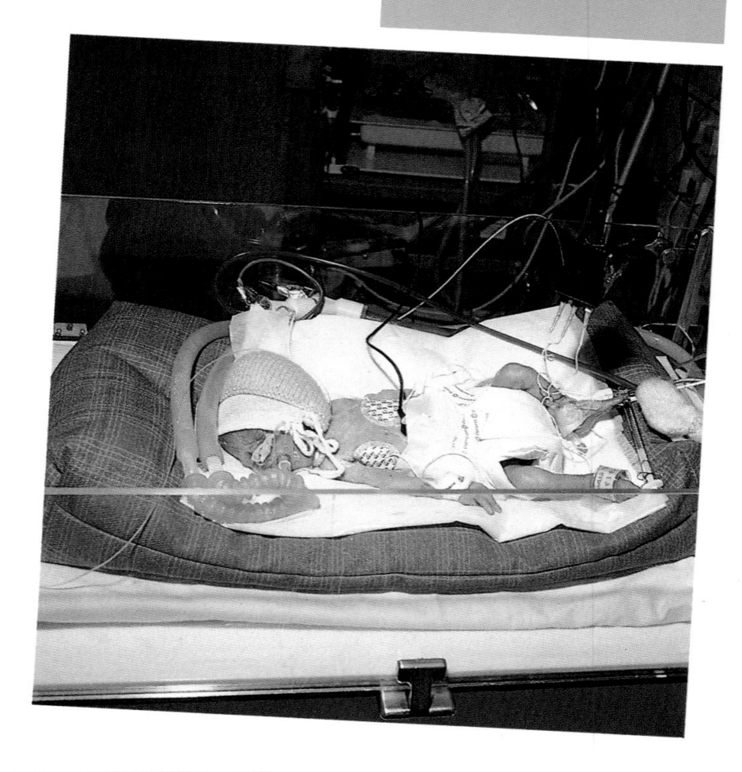

△ This premature baby has been born before its lungs are fully developed, and it cannot breathe properly without help. A ventilator is used to help it to breathe, and monitors are attached to its body to check on heart-rate, temperature and other vital functions.

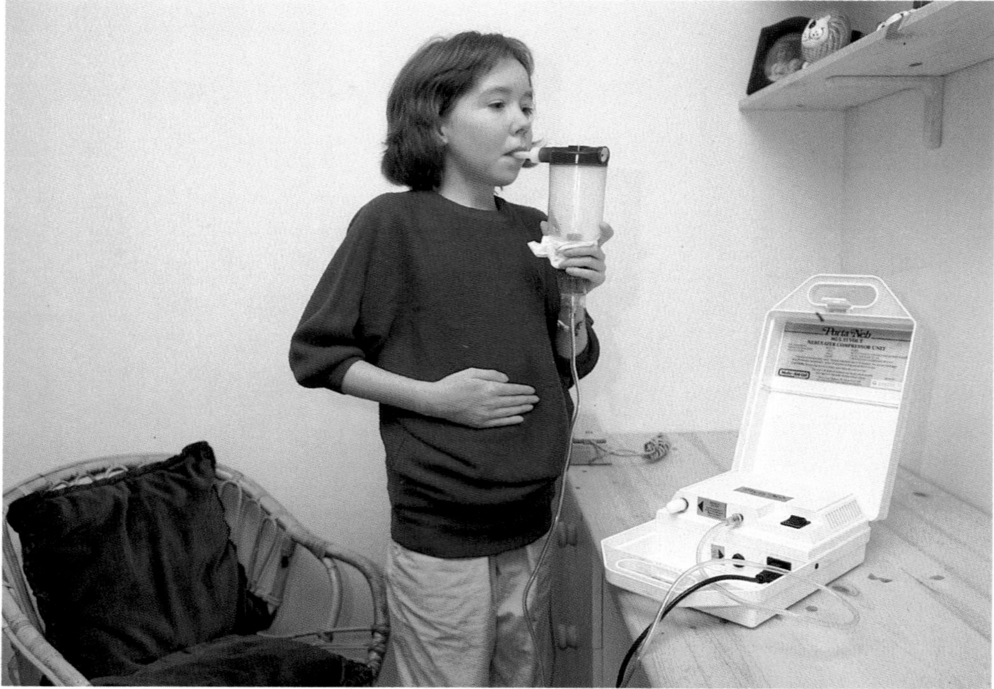

◁ This girl is suffering from cystic fibrosis. To help clear the mucus which could block her lungs, she is inhaling moist air from a machine called a nebuliser. This may be necessary several times each day. She will also be given drugs to prevent lung infections.

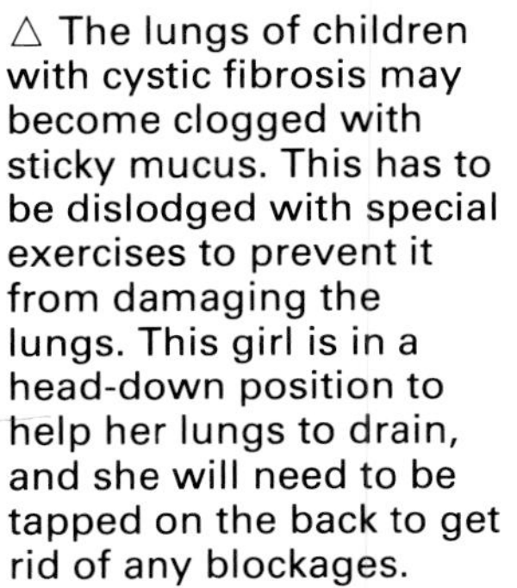

△ The lungs of children with cystic fibrosis may become clogged with sticky mucus. This has to be dislodged with special exercises to prevent it from damaging the lungs. This girl is in a head-down position to help her lungs to drain, and she will need to be tapped on the back to get rid of any blockages.

(top right) Because the effects of her cystic fibrosis are well controlled by treatment, this girl is able to enjoy playing the trumpet. This is useful therapy because it improves breathing.

(bottom right) Many people can now live normal lives after a heart and lung transplant, like this 9-year-old girl.

very difficult to dislodge, and often become infected. Children with cystic fibrosis have to be taught how to dislodge the mucus, and may need to be slapped daily on the back to clear their lungs. A few people with cystic fibrosis or other severe lung diseases are treated with a lung transplant, or sometimes, with a combined heart/lung transplant.

THE HUMAN VOICE

The human body produces sounds by forcing air across the vocal cords in the throat: these vibrate in the airflow to make a sound. You can alter the sound you make in various ways. By bringing the vocal cords closer together and increasing the tension on them, you make your voice higher. Passing more air over them makes the sound louder. But the voice consists of much more complicated actions. The sound rising from the voice box is modified by the throat, tongue, lips and soft palate, and these movements are extremely complicated. If you have ever had an anaesthetic at the dentist, think how difficult it is to talk with your mouth or tongue partly numbed. The quality of the voice is also affected by air escaping up the nose; the sounds you make may well be limited if a cold has blocked your nasal passages.

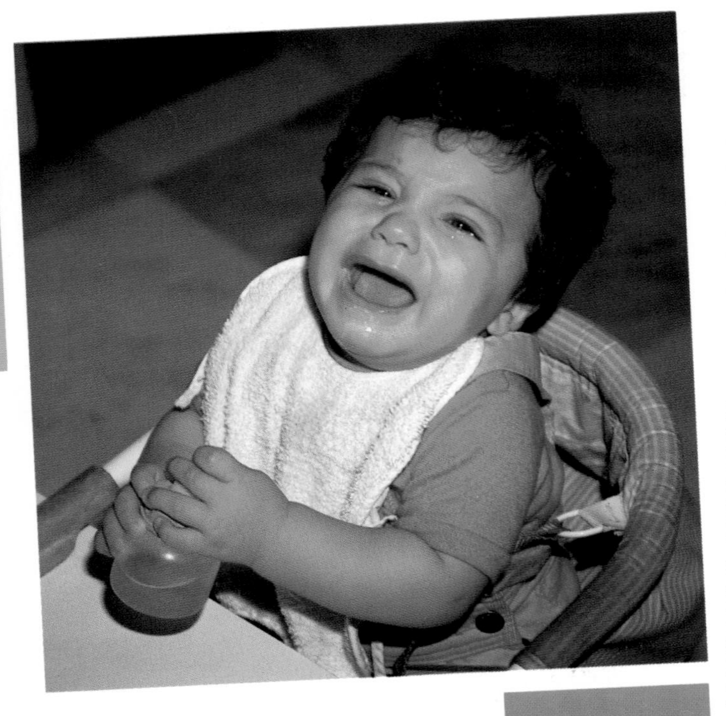

◁ We can convey a message with our voice without using speech. Mothers soon know when their baby is crying in anger, because of hunger, or through distress, just by the type of cry. A baby cannot learn speech until it is able to control its breathing enough to produce words.

△ Opera singing demands a very powerful voice and precise control of breathing. These skills are only acquired after years of training.

GLOSSARY

Air pressure: Although you cannot feel it, air has mass or weight, pressing on every part of your body. As you go higher, the air is thinner, and will not press on your body so much. This is called low pressure.

Allergy: An allergy is a reaction by the body to a usually harmless substance, treating it like a dangerous invader. As a result, a chemical called histamine is produced by the body, and it is this that causes the redness and itching in an allergy.

Alveoli: Alveoli are tiny air sacs in the lungs, with walls so thin that oxygen and carbon dioxide can pass through them.

Bronchi/bronchioles: Air passes in and out of the lungs through a pair of airways branching off the trachea, called bronchi. These branch to form the smallest airways in the lungs called bronchioles.

Capillary: Blood vessels branch to form tiny capillaries. The walls of capillaries are thin so that oxygen and carbon dioxide can pass through them.

Carbon dioxide: This is a waste gas produced by the cells. It dissolves in the blood, and leaves the body through the lungs.

Diaphragm: This muscular sheet divides the chest from the digestive organs in the abdomen. Contraction of the diaphragm causes air to enter the lungs.

Epiglottis: As you swallow, this small flap closes off the entrance to the larynx and airways to prevent food or drink from entering the airways.

Immune system: The body defends itself from dangerous microbes or foreign substances by means of the immune system. This consists of millions of white blood cells which fight infection and clear up damaged body cells.

Larynx: Our voice is produced in the larynx or "Adam's apple". This is a tough box made of cartilage, positioned at the top of the trachea. It contains tightly stretched vocal cords, which vibrate as air passes over them.

Lungs: The lungs are two large spongy organs situated in the chest. They are the main organs of breathing.

Microbe: Many small organisms can attack the body, and these are collectively known as microbes. Most of the microbes causing disease are bacteria or viruses.

Middle ear: The air-filled chamber in the ear mechanism where sound is conveyed and made stronger by three tiny bones.

Mucus: This sticky clear liquid moistens the surface of many organs. In the lungs and the air passages of the nose, mucus traps inhaled dirt so it can be removed harmlessly.

Oxygen: All the living cells of the body need oxygen to break down food substances, releasing energy.

Trachea: Short airway connecting the larynx to the bronchi. It is surrounded by tough hoops of cartilage so it can bend without shutting off the flow of air.

Virus: Tiny organism which often causes colds, 'flu and other types of infection. A virus lives by taking over a living cell and using it as a "factory" to make more viruses.

Vocal cords: Two muscular bands stretched aross the larynx. They vibrate as air passes across them, producing sound.

INDEX

PRINTED IN BELGIUM BY proost INTERNATIONAL BOOK PRODUCTION